Flight

For dreamers everywhere

First published in Great Britain in 2008 by
Frances Lincoln Children's Books, 4 Torriano Mews,
Torriano Avenue, London NW5 2RZ.
www.franceslincoln.com

British Library Cataloguing in Publication Data available on request

ISBN 978-1-84507-674-0

Set in Bembo

Printed in China / Singapore

1 3 5 7 9 8 6 4 2

Night Flight

Michaela Morgan

Illustrated by Erika Pál

F

FRANCES LINCOLN
CHILDREN'S BOOKS

Chapter 1

Danni's new world was a grey world.

Grey streets.

Grey buildings.

Grey rain.

Grey-faced people.

Danni felt grey too.

All the colour had drained from his life.

His new world smelled of fast food and car fumes. And it was cold.

The cold seeped into Danni's skin, down to his bones, into his heart.

He was frozen.

When he allowed himself to think about his real home, his own home, his country and his family, he would feel a rush of panic. What was happening there now?

Then a glow would grow, warmth would surround him. He'd remember the smell of the foods and the fruits, the warm ground beneath his feet, the touch of the sun, the sound of his mother singing.

The memories warmed him. But now they were fading. They said he was in a safe place here. But it was cold and grey.

⭐

The place where Danni lived with his 'aunty' was a tall, grey block. Concrete. Walkways, like rat runs, surrounded it. The lift was grey metal and smelled of pee. Writing was scrawled across the walls.

Much of this scrawl was meaningless to Danni. Many of the words that the gang of kids shouted at him were unknown to him too, but he could understand the tone of their voices. They hated him.

⭐

All day long at school, Danni filled his brain with new words, new ideas, facts, information.

Every day he learnt new things. He'd learnt:

1. Every time you start a new piece of work, you write the date.

2. Then you draw a straight line down the left hand side of the page.

3. And this is called a margin.

4. He'd learnt that he was only allowed to read the books with a blue band stuck on them. Even though there was a red one with a picture of a camel and he would have liked to read that one.

5. He learnt that you stand up straight. Walk don't run. Sit with bottom on the floor.

6. He'd learnt that you were allowed to put things in the bin but you were not allowed to take things out of the bin.

7. He'd learnt that he was useless at spelling.

8. He learnt that if someone poked you in the back, you had to stay quiet. You must not turn round and hit them.

9. Even if they had really hurt you.

10. He'd learnt that if you sat and stared out of the window, this was bad.

11. But if you sat and stared at a bit of paper, this was good.

12. He'd learnt that you sat perfectly still and quiet in the hall when it was assembly.

13. You had to run round and round it when it was P.E.

14. It was very bad if you ran round and round it in assembly. Even if something had frightened you.

15. He'd learnt that you eat your pie with a knife and fork but if you eat your cake with a knife and fork, everyone laughs at you.

16. He learnt that you never EVER run away from a teacher who is shouting at you.

17. You have to stand still and look at your feet.

18. He had learnt that you do not cross bridges until you come to them.

19. But he had never thought of trying to cross a bridge before he came to it.

He had a feeling that none of this made sense.

20. But he had learnt you had to look as if it did and to nod from time to time to show you were listening.

Late in the afternoons, after school had finished, Danni went to the library. It was on his way home, just outside school, just before the shops and only five minutes' walk from the stairs that led to his front door.

He liked the library. It was quiet. Peaceful. The carpets softened all sound. There was no running or screaming or shouting and taunting here - just the quiet sigh of pages turning and the gentle *click click clop* of computer keyboards.

Here he filled his head with pictures and stories: whales and mermaids, elephants and dragons, giants and astronauts ... Sometimes he felt his head was filled to overflowing.

At night in bed, trying to sleep, Danni wished he could fill his heart and soul. He felt an emptiness deep inside him - he was like the hollowed-out skin of some fruit that had had all its juices scooped out. He seemed to have lost his heart somewhere. He couldn't *feel* any more. Everything was muffled. He seemed to be at a distance from everything.

He longed to feel warmth, air, the rays of the sun and the voices of his friends and family,

speaking in a language he knew. Here everything
was so cold and grey and strange. Oh, they tried
to be nice to him. They smiled and they smiled.
They asked him questions. They gave him pieces
of paper. They'd given him warm clothes, a coat,
shoes, socks, a school uniform, a woolly hat.

They'd found him a 'home' and an 'aunty'
to live with. Aunty tried to be nice. She didn't
speak his language but she smiled. A lot.
BIG smiles. She spoke to him in a loud voice

and she asked questions, questions, questions.

"What did you do today, Daniel?"

Danni couldn't help sighing. She was trying to get him to open up. She meant well, but she couldn't even get his name right. Everyone he met twisted his name one way or another. On and on she went with her cheery voice and her big smile.

"How was school, Daniel?"

"Have you made any friends yet, Daniel?"

"Do you like fish fingers, Daniel?"

Danni struggled to find the words to ask his own questions:

"Will I stay here ever and ever?"

"You send me back? Or keep me?"

"When you go find my family?"

"Will you let come over here?"

No one ever gave him an answer. They just went quiet and said: "We'll cross that bridge when we get to it."

Before bedtime, in the cramped living-room, breathing in the stuffy unmoving air, Danni pedalled an exercise bike.

This had been a good find. He had seen it twisted and abandoned in a skip in the street. It seemed that someone had grown so frustrated with it that they had thrown it from a great height. Danni had rescued and restored it.

He had always liked rescuing and restoring. It was what he used to do back home. With his father he would wander and search. They would return from their wanderings with their arms heaped with finds. Sometimes they would come back dragging huge sacks of stuff behind them.

Sometimes they'd be pushing an enormous heap in front of them. And then they'd start sifting and sorting and thinking and discussing and polishing and shaping, and little by little a new something would appear before them.

These old rusty wheels and this plank would make a cart.

This bunch of tangled wire would make a toy.

These ragged coloured bags would become rugs or bags – or a model chicken!

In Danni's new neighbourhood, the skips and tips were always bulging with things that still had plenty of life in them. He'd found a chair. He'd found nearly an entire chess set with a fold-out board, still in its box. He'd found a lamp shaped like a banana.

When he saw the twisted exercise bike, Danni knew he could restore it.

He dragged it up to the flat and convinced his 'aunty' he could make it as good as new.

"And then we can sell it," she said.

Now the bike worked perfectly, but it remained unsold in the small living-room and every night Danni pedalled it. He pedalled furiously, faster and faster. His legs raced round until he grew breathless. He pedalled and pedalled faster, faster. And, of course, he moved not an inch.

He had spent so long moving to get to this grey country. There had been that first wild panic ride, then the jolting cars, the trains, that awful boat, the crammed truck.

"Don't think," he told himself. "Just pedal, just pedal."

★ ☆ ★

Danni liked to tire himself out in the hope that deep, undisturbed sleep would follow. Then he tried to soothe himself to sleep by imagining chess games in his head. The queen moves here. *Click*. The knight protects her. *Clop*. The pawns all gather around. The squares go black, white, black, white in a regular pattern. *Clip clop, clip clop*, step by careful step. It can all be worked out.

When Danni closed his eyes and the blackness surrounded him again, he found it difficult to breathe. When he curled up to sleep, he had flashbacks to the cramped lorry he'd spent so long travelling in. He would snap his eyes open and spread his limbs wide to reassure himself that he was not trapped. "It's all right. It's OK," he told himself. "You're safe. Just breathe calmly. Breathe. Breathe."

But it didn't work. Not the frantic pedalling. Not the planning out of his imaginary chess game. Not his attempts to relax. Nothing soothed him.

Danni had terrible nightmares.

Chapter 2

Danni's head ached from the shrapnel of his days. Today there had been that fearsome scurry home. Taunts and jibes followed him home most evenings. He suffered the looks. The stale air. The cruel words lobbed at him like stones.

A group of kids in his school had ganged up against him. It had started on his very first day at Upperton Middle School. Miss Simmonds, the teacher, made him stand at the front of the class and introduced him.

"This is Dan," she said.

She got his name wrong. They all did. But they all got it wrong in different ways. There were so many versions of Danni's name now, he feared that one day he would forget what his real name was.

Miss Simmonds smiled and asked him some questions.

Danni blinked. He didn't understand most of her words. He didn't have the vocabulary to answer the few questions he'd understood.

"Don't worry," she said. "You'll soon pick it up."

He blinked again, confused. It was all so strange. "SOON PICK IT UP!" she repeated, and he had bent down to look for whatever it was he was to pick up. And they laughed.

The whole class laughed, but particularly Kriss and Keifer and Kevin - the three beefy-looking boys on the table where he was told to sit.

"Reading the baby books, are we?"

From then on, Kriss was always the first to start on him.

"Can't read very well, can we?" The other two were quick to follow.

"Haven't picked it up yet, then?"

And worse.

Words were hissed at him as they passed in the corridors. Nudgings and jostlings stopped just short of pushing him over.

And then there were the looks.

Chapter 3

Kriss practised his looks at home. In front of his smeary bathroom mirror he searched for the right look – the one that would inspire fear, and earn respect.

He tried scowling through half-open slits of eyes.

He tried pulling his lip up into a sneer.

He raised an eyebrow and tried to look cool and superior.

He lowered his eyebrows in the hope of looking fierce.

The sudden violent hammering on the bathroom door burst his fantasies. His dad was not the sort to wait patiently.

Kriss rearranged his features and opened the door. The face he presented to the glowering bulk that was his father was a humble face. It was the face of a downtrodden puppy, desperate to please.

"Sorry, Dad..." he started, but he got no further before the usual slap made his ears ring.

☆☆☆

At school, Kriss shared his table with Keifer and Kevin. They were his mates. He was their leader. They were the three biggest kids in the class. Not the quickest. Not the brightest. But definitely the biggest.

Kriss called his gang *The Three Ks* or *KKK* and they didn't take no rubbish from no one. There had been a time at another school – when he was much smaller – when *he'd* been the butt of jokes.

He used to hang around his teacher. He tried to follow her home. Once, without thinking, he called her 'mummy' and tried to kiss her. His ears burned red with shame at that long-ago memory.

Other kids, back then, had started to call him Kisstopher instead of Krisstopher. They'd said: "Give us a kiss, Kriss!" and "Give Miss a kiss!" and "Give Kriss a miss!" "Kissy Krissy!" Stuff like that. But that was long ago. He'd learnt how to deal with it. So now, even though he and Kevin and Keifer were made to sit at the Dolphin table and be specially helped by Mrs 'Saddo' Sadler, *nobody* laughed at him. Nobody laughed at him now.

In Krisstopher's class the tables were all named after animals and fish. Their teacher, Miss Simmonds, pointed out that a dolphin was a highly intelligent, smiling, good-natured sea creature and so it was really good to be a dolphin. But Kriss knew that the Dolphin table was in fact the bottom table and that - far from being highly intelligent, smiling and good-natured – he and the other two K's were surly, sulking and thick as bricks. But now there was someone lower down the pecking order.

One day Miss Simmonds had come in and stood an odd-looking, gangly boy in front of them. "This is Dan," she'd said.

And then she went into her long, l...o...n...g

introduction, but the Three K's weren't listening – they were looking. They were looking at Danni.

"What does he think he looks like?" Kriss hissed. "What catalogue did he find that get-up in?"

The new boy was wearing grey trousers ironed to have a crease you could have cut cheese with. He had a white shirt starched so stiff it could have stood up by itself. A tie – a full-length dangling one! Black leather shoes – very shiny and tightly laced up. And a blazer. A blazer!

"Getta load of that," jeered Kriss. "It's the dork from the *Back to School* ads!" The other two Ks sneered obediently.

☆☆☆

Now, every afternoon after school, the three Ks lurked in wait for Danni. Away from their teachers they could really get stuck into him.

Danni had taken to dodging into the library to avoid them. At first he'd hung around on the edges of the library pretending to read the notice-board, but now he went straight in, sat down, picked up a book and drank it in.

He couldn't read the words, all back to front and in strange stiff, spiky letters, but he loved the pictures – and the colours. Oh the colours! Like exotic fruit they blossomed before his eyes. Raspberry red, bruised berry purple, mango, papaya and orange. He drank the colours in, taking great gulps of cool, fresh green, sipping at the heavenly blue, swallowing down the sparkling silver and molten sunshine.

★ ★ ★

Outside the library, the Three Ks grew tired of waiting.

"Leave it," said Kriss. "He'll keep till tomorrow."

"Later," Keifer chimed in.

"Later." Kevin was always quick to agree with the other two.

They split up and drifted home. Keifer to his mammoth plate of burgers and beans, Kevin to his fish fingers and chips, and Kriss to whatever he could find. His dad wouldn't be in for hours.

Kriss let himself into his flat and, ferreting about the cupboards, emerged triumphantly with a multi-pack of crisps. Ten small, crinkly bags of variously flavoured crisps lay before him: prawn cocktail, cheese and onion, salt and vinegar, tomato sauce, tangy barbeque, tasty tandoori...

"I'll just eat one bag," Kriss told himself. "Dad'll never notice."

But he was ravenous and had soon wolfed down the entire jumbo pack. His mouth was powdery with prawn cocktail and cheese and onion flavour. His throat felt clogged and he still didn't feel full. No matter how much he ate, he always had an empty feeling. He carefully crumpled the empty bags up small and stuffed them at the bottom of the bin, burying them behind old dried-up teabags and empty lager cans. He didn't want to give his dad any reason for being mad at him again.

He turned the TV on and slumped in front of it. Cartoon mayhem exploded on to the screen, crashes and chases, screams and taunts. Kriss lay back while it washed over him.

"I'll sort that Danny-boy loser out tomorrow," he muttered to himself. "Tomorrow."

★ ★ ★

Tomorrow – another day at school. But this was to be a different day. Miss Simmonds tried to explain it to Danni. She spoke clearly and loudly as if he was deaf or stupid.

"School VISIT," she'd explained. "DAY OUT!" Danni didn't understood. He was still learning new words every day.

"WE GO IN A BUS FROM SCHOOL – YOU AND ALL THE CLASS. WE GO TO VISIT CITY FARM. VISIT ANIMALS. UNDERSTAND?"

"Yes," Danni had nodded. He understood 'go' and 'visit' and 'city' and 'farm'. He understood 'animals'. He didn't see how these things connected, but he would wait and see.

She waved a piece of paper at him – people were always waving pieces of paper at him, papers closely printed with words he didn't know.

"ASK MUM OR DAD TO SIGN PERMISSION FORM" she'd added, and then she paused.

Did she understand that he had no idea where his mum and dad were? They might be dead. They might be hurt. They might be struggling to get to him – perhaps they were getting closer and closer to him every day. Danni liked to imagine them moving towards him step by step. He liked to picture them like the pieces on a chess board, advancing slowly, planning their strategy, avoiding pitfalls, getting closer and closer to him with each move. But probably they weren't.

Danni knew only too well how difficult it was to get out of his old country. He knew how difficult it was to get into this new one. It had been a nightmare getting here and now there was talk of sending him back.

Miss Simmonds put the permission form into Danni's hand. She smiled brightly and continued, "ASK YOUR AUNTY TO SIGN FORM.

BRING PACKED LUNCH."

Then she moved off to deal with a gang of troublemakers down the corridor. It was the Three K's up to their tricks again.

They had many tricks. Most of them simply relied on being bigger and bulkier than the other kids. But recently they had come up with a new trick.

They'd taken to cutting bits out of Kriss's dad's newspaper and sticking them on the wall. The teachers and some of the other kids ripped them down and the wastepaper bins were now full of strips of headlines with their talk of waves of refugees, tides of refugees, floods of refugees. There was fear of a deluge.

SEND 'EM PACKING! screamed one headline....

ASYLUM ANARCHY ranted another.

INVASION MUST BE STOPPED said a third.

Scraps and tatters of other words – like *Threat* and *Bogus* and *Plague*, lay coiled snake-like in the basket, waiting to bite.

Danni was just a small part of this human flotsam and jetsam. He was a refugee and the

block of grey flats was his refuge. Sometimes it seemed more like a lair.

At night, the sounds of sirens whooped around him. There was shouting and scuffling in the street below and the yellow, monster-eyed street lamps bathed his room in a sickly glow.

Each night it took him a longer time to drift into an edgy sleep.

Each morning he woke, his head still full of the remnants of the nightmare in which he was running, running, running...

In Danni's nightmares there were echoes of his terrifying night flight all that time ago.

It was the night the soldiers had come banging and shouting at his door, and he and his family and all their neighbours had run and run. First down tarmac streets, then down dusty lanes, finally down stinking alleys. He'd been fast and he'd been young and he'd been lucky, and he'd scrambled on to the back of the truck bouncing away, the soldiers behind him growing smaller and smaller in the distance.

In his dream, he reached out his hand to pull the others up behind him, but his arm was too short and they were too slow and, like the soldiers, his family grew smaller and smaller, and finally faded away.

Now other images were creeping into his nightmare. His sleep was peopled with more and more shadowy creatures shouting and hissing things he couldn't quite hear or understand. They threw coiled strips of paper insults at him. He ran, and they pursued him, getting ever closer as he raced frantically down smaller and smaller alleys to escape. He couldn't run fast enough.

His lungs were burning with the effort. His legs were collapsing under him. A bird or a plane – or something – swept by high above him.

If only he could fly too.

Chapter 4

On Tuesday morning Danni sat with the rest of
the class as the register was called. As usual, he was
exhausted, drained by his uneasy sleep and
muddied by his nightmare. Then, one by one, two
by two or in little clumps, the kids jostled on to
the bus for the class visit.

Danni had a double seat to himself. He
expected this. He wasn't great company and he
wasn't one of any gang. While the rest of the kids
were all identically relaxed in their uniforms of
trainers and baggy shirts, he stood out in his crisp
outfit, his tie neatly knotted, his shoes shiny.
His aunty thought it was important to look smart
at school.

★ ☆ ★

At home, in his own country, Danni had always

been smart. Whatever was going on, he had tried to keep himself dust-free. It hadn't been easy. It hadn't been easy to concentrate in school with all that was going on in his homeland, but he had tried.

Now, in this new school, he worked hard but he struggled with the language and he struggled to find something he could say to all these people who had such different lives from him. What could he say that they would understand? What could he possibly say? There were things too terrible to talk of. He had retreated into almost complete silence when he'd first arrived in this country, and in this silence he stayed.

Strangers looked at him and saw a gangly, strange-looking boy who avoiding looking in their eyes. They heard his speech limited to a 'yes' or a 'no' or, more usually, 'don't know' and assumed he was sulking or simple-minded. Now he sat on the school bus in his usual silence and looked at the city streets rolling by on the short journey to the City Farm.

He was beginning to understand where he was going. Well, he understood the words, but he had no clue why people would keep farm animals just to visit. Like visiting relatives? A strange idea. A strange country.

But when Danni got to the farm, he felt a sense of familiarity. Everyone tumbled off the bus, took in the sights and the sounds and the smells and went "Phew!" and "What a pong!"

There was much giggling and messing about and pushing, but Danni stood completely still and breathed.

He breathed in the comforting animal smells – straw and dust and feathers. With each familiar musky waft of goat he began to feel himself relax.

Then:

"Bet you EAT those where you come from, don't you, Danny-boy?" Kriss and a gaggle of boys pointed at the goat.

Danni nodded. Yes, he did eat them.

The boys sneered. One pretended to be sick.

A cheeky hen pecked at Danni's feet. Danni pointed at the hen and looked at the boys. "You eat. Yes?"

The boys shrugged, but stuck to their taunts. "Bet you eat horse too. There's one over there

looks like he's gonna peg out any time. Yum yum for you."

They rubbed their stomachs, licked their lips and sniggered at a grey horse standing in the shadows. It was dusty and tired looking. It looked about to drop.

"Ah, you've noticed poor old Stump." A man dressed in a City Farm sweatshirt approached them. He introduced himself.

"I'm Tim O'Brien. I'm in charge here and these are my assistants, Gary and Kate. And that poor beast..." he pointed to the horse "... that's Stump. She's in a bit of a bad way."

Lia, one of the girls in Danni's class, went over to pat Stump. The horse made a scary *harrumphing* noise and shied away. "What's the matter with him?" Lia asked.

"*Her*," said the farm man. "Stump is a mare."

"Silly mare," Kriss sniggered.

"We don't really know what's the matter with her," Mr O'Brien continued. "She was found wandering on wasteland so we took her in. But it doesn't look as if she's got long for this world. The vet's coming to see her later."

Lia put out her hand to try to pat the mare again. Then she recoiled.

"*Eee-uch!*" she grimaced. "It's got a big ugly wart on its head!"

"That's why we call her Stump!" said Gary, the assistant. "Never seen anything like it before – it's some kind of growth. I wouldn't touch it, if I were you."

Lia shuddered. "No way am I going anywhere near that scabby thing. Let's go and look at the lambs."

"Be back here in one hour," Miss Simmonds waved a pile of worksheets at them. "Answer as many questions as you can, and remember: PUT YOUR NAME ON YOUR WORK."

They all collected their work sheets and went on their way. Miss Simmonds hurried after them.

Only Danni stayed behind.

He gazed at the scabby horse: a lost creature, wandering and tired. He knew exactly how that felt.

He put out a tentative hand.

Chapter 5

The horse gazed at him. Huge, weary brown eyes seemed to look deep into Danni. The horse twitched its ears, as if it was waiting to hear something.

Danni stared back.

They gazed in silence at each other for some time – for a long time.

The other kids were out of sight now, and still Danni stared into those sad, tired eyes.

Then: "Hello," Danni murmured – but not hello in this new English language. He spoke in his own language – the real language, the language of his mother and father. His own voice sounded rusty to him.

"Are you weary?" he asked. He could speak his own language to this animal – which probably understood no languages at all – or all languages the same.

"Try to relax," Danni urged the horse. "Breathe." This is what he told himself each night as he tried to sleep.

The horse dipped her head towards Danni's outstretched hand.

Danni patted it timidly. "Will you bite?" he asked. "Are you afraid?"

The horse nudged her nose against Danni's hand. Now, it was the horse who was stroking Danni. He just stood still as the mare moved her dusty head up and down his dry hands.

"You feel cold," said Danni. "You are dusty. You have travelled far, perhaps?"

The horse moved her head up and down.

"Are your bones aching? Is your mouth dusty? Does it taste of ashes?" asked Danni. "Would you like clean water?"

He took a bucket over to the tap and filled it. Water frothed fresh as it gushed into the bucket. Sparkles of light danced in it and Danni felt a rush of – what was it? Familiarity? Comfort? Recognition. He brought the water back to the horse. The horse drank.

He picked up a handful of oats from the horse's feeder. The horse bent her head and ate.

∗⟡∗

Some time later, Miss Simmonds came bustling back. She was hot, she was cross, she had a million things to do at the same time and her shoes hurt. She'd given everyone a worksheet, explained everything in detail – twice to some, three times to Kriss and his lot. She was looking forward to sitting in the shade and taking her shoes off.

Then, when she'd made her final check on her flock, she had realised she was one student short. One lost – already! She'd had a moment of panic, then realised that Danni had failed to move on with the rest of the class.

She clutched her wodge of papers and set off back to find him. She glanced irritably at her watch and started to shout. "Get a move on, Danni..." she began. "You haven't even taken your worksheet..."

Then she stopped.

She saw Danni standing still, but with his head, for once, raised – and was he *talking*? He was. He was talking – *talking* to that scabby horse! How long had she been trying to get through to him? She'd tried everything she could think of to get him to speak! And now, ten minutes alone with a dusty old nag, the scabbiest horse in the world, and he was... well he was making some sort of crooning, clicking, murmuring sound – like no language she'd ever heard.

She stopped in her tracks and watched.

✫✫✫

Tim O'Brien, the farm man, was on his way past. He stopped too.

"Well, well..." he said, "...that student of yours must be something special. Poor old Stump doesn't usually take to people. We've been trying to get her to trust us ever since we found her. Now look – she's taking food from his hand!"

Miss Simmonds looked thoughtful. She shuffled her papers. "Have you got time for a little chat, Mr O'Brien?"

42

"I was just off for my break," he replied. "Fancy a cup of tea?"

✫✫✫

Miss Simmonds sipped at her mug of tea. "Mr O'Brien..." she started.

"Tim," he said.

Miss Simmonds pinked. "Tim then... that boy... his name's Dan... well, he's a bit of a problem – I mean a *challenge* for me."

She took a deep breath. "You see we have this new project – a bit like Work Experience, only for younger kids. Another of the Government's

bright ideas," she sighed, and continued. "Each of our students is supposed to spend two days with one of their parents or relatives at work. Well, obviously, it's been hard to find safe placements for our lot. Many of our parents don't have jobs. We started saying it was to be only mothers and fathers, then we went on to uncles and aunties, brothers, sisters, grandmas, mother's best friends, second cousins twice removed... We've scraped the barrel now... but we just can't find anyone to take Dan. He's got no family at all here. His foster mum has no job and there's no one else willing to take him. He hardly speaks at all. His English is very poor. He's timid, withdrawn. So he's a bit difficult to place and, well, I wonder if ..."

"You want us to have him here?" said Tim. "I don't know..."

"The City Farm – and you – have had a long connection with our school. You're one of the Governors. You've taken assemblies. We know this would be a really safe place for him. And Dan does seem to have a way with the horse," said Miss Simmonds, a little too brightly. "Maybe other animals too. His lack of language wouldn't be a problem with them, would it...?"

☆☆☆

Two cups of tea and twenty minutes later and it was all settled.

Miss Simmonds tried to explain it to Danni. She gave him a piece of paper and began to talk enthusiastically and quickly.

"WORK EXPERIENCE PROJECT," she pointed to the paper. "All the students in your year do it. EVERYONE. Do you understand? Two days you WORK here. Thursday and Friday. You're very LUCKY. Do you know how lucky you are? Mr O'Brien has been very kind."

Danni blinked at the piece of paper in his hands. There was a silence. Miss Simmonds shuffled her papers uneasily. In the background, Kriss and Keifer sniggered.

The farm man took over the conversation. He offered his hand to Danni. "I'm Tim," he said. "Tim O'Brien. You're Danny - right? You like the horse? The horse," Tim pointed to it. "You like?"

Danni nodded.

"She's called Stump. It's because of that."
He pointed to the hard growth. It looked as if
something had snapped on her head. "Stump is
very ill - old and sick and tired and... something
else. We don't know what's the matter with her.
It's probably something to do with that growth.
She needs looking after - lots of care and
attention. Will you care for her?"

Tim, Danni and the horse stood and stared at
each other.

Tim let the silence fall, then patted Danni's

arm and repeated, "Will you care for Old Stump?"

Danni raised his head and looked at Tim.

He took a deep breath and said one whole sentence.

Quite clearly he said: "Her name is Moonlight."

Chapter 6

"It's not fair," Kriss muttered. "I get to work in a poxy bucket factory and he gets to hang out in a park all day. It's just like my dad says – they steal our jobs."

"Yeah," Keifer agreed. "Started early, haven't you, Danny-boy."

"That's enough!" Miss Simmonds was crisp. "Back on to the coach and I don't want to hear another word from you three. And you," she looked at Kriss, "you take another worksheet and start again. This time without the so-called witticisms."

"Always picks on me, doesn't she?" Kriss mumbled. "And *he* gets the top job, the big smile, the pat on the head. He hasn't even started his worksheet. He hasn't even *taken* a worksheet. And did she say anything to him?"

He slouched on his seat at the back of the bus

and gave a swift kick to the seat in front of him. Danni winced, but he didn't turn round, didn't say anything. He just kept his head down, his mouth closed and his mind blank.

✳ ✵ ✵

The next Thursday, Danni walked to the farm park. He followed the map and directions given to him by Tim. He set off very early when the air was fresher and the cars fewer. It took him over an hour to walk there. Miss Simmonds had tried to explain: "You take a BUS," she said "A 22 or a 34."

"Or a 53," Tim had added.

Danni looked at both of them. "I like walk," he said. "I like move."

Undaunted, Miss Simmonds carried on. "You get off the bus just outside the gate and you must arrive by 9 o'clock. You work from 9 o'clock till 3.30, Thursday and Friday."

But Danni went on Thursday and Friday and he went on Saturday and Sunday too. He went very early. He stayed as late as he was allowed.

It was nearly dark by the time he set off home.

Every day when he went into the Farm Park, he stood stone-still and listened.

He breathed in deeply.

Then he went to the stables. The tired horse seemed glad to see him. She would raise her head.

Danni spent hours brushing her. Hours and hours, slowly, rhythmically,

Swoosh

Swoosh

Swoosh

and slowly, slowly her dingy grey coat regained some of its lost sheen.

Danni brushed her tail and mane,

Swoosh

Swoosh.

The regular rhythmic movements soothed both of them.

Slowly, slowly her mane and tail untangled.

Her tail started to twitch playfully.

Her mane started to move in the breeze.

Danni oiled the horse's hooves.

They started to shine.

And as he brushed and combed and stroked and oiled, Danni talked and sang.

He remembered old songs his mother had sung to him and he sang those to the horse.

He remembered stories from his old country and he told them to the horse.

He remembered words his mother had used to comfort him when he had been hurt. He whispered these words to the horse and the horse seemed comforted. So did Danni.

"What have those eyes seen, to make them so sad?" Danni asked the horse. "Where have these feet been, that they have become so sore?"

He picked out the stones from Moonlight's hooves.

"*Whoaa*," he said. "Some of these have been here a long time. Have you been wandering for a long time? Like me. Are you hurting? Like me? There. It's out now. Better?"

He rubbed lemon-smelling lotion on to the horse's legs.

"Tired muscles?" he asked. "Have you been cramped up in a lorry? In a tiny space, not able to move? Hardly able to breathe? Travelling, travelling with no idea where you were? Your heart hurting with fear... afraid? I know... I know..."

Danni soothed the horse. He sang and crooned and talked to her. "Your eyes look so tired. What have you seen? What has happened to you? Can you tell me?"

The horse shook her head, scattering a small cloud of flies that were gathering around her head.

"Ah yes," said Danni. "Tales too terrible to tell. Memories buzzing round your head like flies. Shake them off. But you know they will swarm around you again. Sometimes they bite.

"When I started my journey," Danni told the horse, "I thought there was nothing worse than leaving my mother and father behind. My brothers, the baby sister I hardly knew. What could be worse than that, I thought, and then..."

Danni shook his head, but continued: "In one of the trucks I travelled in there were many, many people. Too many. Mostly men and boys, but there was one man with his wife and a little baby.

That baby was a bit like my little sister, you know... it cried. Not a lot, but enough. Enough for the man who was in charge of us to grow angry. 'Why bring a wife?' he hissed. 'Why a baby? It will cost us our lives. If they hear it they, will find us – and what then?' The woman made herself small and hushed the baby.

"But it was no good. The next day that baby was gone and that woman had the look that mad people get. 'Have they taken your baby away?' I whispered, but she did not speak. Her eyes had lost their life... like yours..." Danni rubbed the horse's forehead "Like your eyes, they were – old and tired.

"That woman was the next to go. I don't know what happened to her. She was just one of many people who just... disappeared..."

✱✰✪

Danni found all the old scars and scabs on the weary horse and touched them gently with lotions and ointments.

"Another one..." he would say. "Oh, red

54

and raw... There, there now... better... no more ache... no more pain..."

Danni stroked and soothed, soothed and stroked and he talked and talked and talked. His voice was sounding less rusty. He was beginning to feel warm and alive at last.

The ice in his heart was melting.

Chapter 7

Tim O'Brien brought the vet to visit. "Old Stump is looking much better now, isn't she?" he said.

The sense of desolate dinginess had left her. The horse looked fresher, more alive.

"She is looking better," said the vet, "but still..." He clicked his tongue and shook his head.

"We can't expect miracles. She can't last much longer."

The vet turned to Danni. "You're doing a very good job, though, young man. Old Stump has never looked so good."

"Moonlight," said Danni.

Tim explained "Dan thinks the mare is called Moonlight because..." A pause. "Why do you think she's called Moonlight?"

Danni touched the horse's grey coat. "Cloud," he said. After all his hard work, a dull shine was beginning to break through. "Behind cloud," Danny pointed to the dull gleam, "is moonlight."

"Ah!" said Tim. "Stump was always just Moonlight obscured by clouds. I see!" He smiled broadly.

Danni smiled back – a quick flash of a smile.

"We called her Stump," Tim spoke to the vet, "because of this." He pointed to the growth on the horse's head.

Danni nodded. "Like shell. Sea-shell," he said.

Tim O'Brien smiled again, and patted Danni's arm. "You have the soul of a poet, Dan," he said. "You see the magic in everything."

Chapter 8

Hour followed hour, day followed day.

Swoosh swoosh, oil on gleam.

Swoosh swoosh, shimmer on shine.

Dust, old hair, dried mud, caked dirt all loosened, fell away and were replaced by a faint glimmer, which grew each day.

"Soon," said Danni, "you will shine like the moon."

With the slow pace, the regular rhythm, the horse relaxed. And as the horse relaxed, so did Danni. He felt moments of stillness, of peace, of something like happiness. The oil and the creams seemed to rub off on him too. The horse and Danni healed each other.

Words tumbled out of Danni now: bright, new words from his new country, snippets of sad songs from his old country, snatches of soothing songs, lullabies his mother had sung. Fragments of long-lost stories resurfaced. His dreams and memories came creeping back, peeking out at the light. Whispered words of consolation or encouragement tiptoed back to him, and Danni passed them on to the horse.

The days grew golden. But it couldn't last.

✶✶✶

In no time at all, Miss Simmonds was there clutching more papers and Mr O'Brien was signing them and then they were both talking to Danni.

"We're very pleased with your work," said Miss Simmonds. "PLEASED! You've done well on your work experience but it's over now. FINISHED! You understand? BACK TO SCHOOL ON MONDAY. Yes? Back to NORMAL."

Mr O'Brien touched Danni's shoulder. "Come and visit any weekend, Dan. We'll be glad to see you. So will Old Stump."

The horse stood in the bright sunshine. Her mane lifted in the spring breeze. She seemed to nod her head.

Chapter 9

Monday morning. School. Back to normal. It was the usual hurly-burly. The jostling, the running, banging doors and screaming children. Danni felt himself shrink back into his nightmare. The hurrying, the grabbing and the running and the shouting... like a replay of that terrible night...

He had made his escape in the night. He had faded into the dark. He had scrambled on to the truck and then he was off, bouncing, careering, flying away into the night – and his face was one of many. His eyes darting around desperately searching – like all the others. His voice screaming out – one of many screaming unheard. "No, stop, stop! My mother! My father! Wait for them. Wait for them!"

In school now, Danni was like a snail. Coiled in his shell he peered out, then crept along trying to stay in the shadows, trying not to be noticed and stamped on.

No such luck. They spotted him straight away. The KKK's turned on him.

"Enjoyed our little skive down on the farm, have we?" That was Kriss, but Keifer and Kevin were quickly there and others drifted along following the current. They began to circle round him like sharks.

"Oh, leave him alone," said Lia, but they had their teeth into him now. "Managed to get a cushy little number, didn't he!"

"We end up in boring offices and poxy factories – and who gets the cushy job? Danny-boy!"

"He can hardly speak."

"Can't write! Can't read!"

"Retard!"

"Can't do nothing, but he gets the job! We're not good enough, eh?"

"Started nicking our jobs already, innit?"

"Needs teaching a lesson? Eh?"

"Eh!"

"Eh!"

With each 'Eh,' they jabbed a finger at him.

Sharper each time. Harder each time. Until he was being pushed around from one to the other bouncing between them like a pinball on a machine. It was building up to real pushes and thumps.Harder and harder, faster and faster.

"It's not worth getting into trouble," said one of the boys. "Cool it!"

But on they went... and on. A crowd had gathered around him now. There was jeering, chanting.

"Fight! Fight! Fight!

Faces loomed all around Danni – red faces, spotty faces, white faces, brown faces, grey faces. Close, close, closer.

Then the bell rang.

"Catch ya later, infiltrator!" Kriss sniggered at his own wit.

They drifted off.

✳✳✳

All week long it went on – hissed asides, casual bumpings, snatches of *Old Macdonald Had A Farm*. Kriss had invented a new version of the song. He and his gang never missed a chance to chant:

Old Macdanny had a farm
Phew-ee phewy-poo...

They held their noses as Danni passed.

✳✳✳

Every day the same. School. Danni scuttling along corridors, keeping his head down, keeping an eye out for the gang of three that dogged his steps. Waiting until all was clear at the end of the day. Then a quick scurry across the road to the library – a stepping-stone on the way home each day and a welcome sanctuary.

The woman at the library desk looked up at Danni as he came in. She recognised him and smiled, then carried on with her work.

He made his way to the children's section. There were several boxes of big books with coloured pictures. By the tiny chairs placed near them, Danni guessed they were meant for younger children, but he loved them: bright, bright colour, and the pictures, as well as feeding his eyes, seemed to feed his spirit. They helped him to understand the stories too.

The last book he'd looked at was about a snowman. He couldn't believe it! White stuff would fall from the sky and children would run out into it. They would make little footprints in the snow. They could be the first to leave a footprint in the crispness that was new snow. They could make round white men out of it!

When the library lady came by, she looked over Danni's shoulder.

"Have you ever made a snowman?" she asked.

So it was true – they really did make men out of the snow!

"I remember making them myself," she went on. "We made fantastic snowmen – even better than that one in the picture. I loved those snowmen! Every year – or nearly – a new one, each better than the last. One was really special. He had a top hat – like that one in the picture. But by the morning he had disappeared as if by magic. We couldn't even find the hat!"

Danni went back to the book with even more fascination.

Today the lady brought him two new books.

"Just arrived!" she said "Brand new!" She put the new books down near him.

"We don't get all that many new books nowadays," she said. "It's a special day!"

Danni picked one up.

It smelt so fresh. The pages were clean and shiny and unblemished. He was the first person to turn its pages. He smiled - it was as if he was

the child in the snowman book, making the first footprint in the snow.

He leafed over the pages. It was a book of myths and tales. There were pictures of gods and goddesses, of mountains and seas and monsters and... there was a picture of flying horse. There was a double-page picture of a horse flying high in the sky. High, high over tiny cities, tiny mountains, tinier people. The sky was bright blue and the horse... the horse was pure white.

Danni picked up the second book. He opened the crisp first page and there again – a horse! A horse looking back at him. It had gentle eyes, a flowing mane and... and a long sea-shell growth on his head. It was like Moonlight, but the sea-shell growth was much longer and shining and beautiful.

Danni looked at the library lady. "I know horse like that," he said.

"That's no ordinary horse," she said. "That's a unicorn. It's magic."

"Look!" She turned to the central section of the book.

The page was shiny, glossy. There were

beautiful pictures of gleaming white unicorns tossing silver manes as they galloped beside blue seas, grazed in green fields, lingered by waterfalls against starlit skies. On each of the unicorns' heads shone a long, shining, sea-shell-like spear.

There were columns and columns of crisp black print and on top of it all, in lilac-blue squirly writing, the word *Unicorn*.

It was very airy writing. It seemed to be flying across the page.

Danni made himself focus on the crisp black words and the difficult task of squeezing some meaning out of them.

It wasn't easy, but by concentrating fiercely, linking them to the pictures and guessing a great deal, he learnt that:

1. The unicorn is a mythical beast.

2. It has been known by many names in many places, in many times.

3. In the Orient they call it *Ki Lin*.

4. In Arabia they call it *Karkadahn*.

5. It is a creature of magic that flourishes in beauty and purity, innocence and love.

6. It cannot flourish without these things.

Danni traced his fingers over the words, trying to coax out more of the meaning, but much of it remained cloudy. Some of the words were unknown to him. *Flourish*? What was *flourish*? To be like a flower? Ah yes – to open up like a flower in the sunshine. To open up, a flower needed sunlight and rain. Without these things it would wither, it would die. So if a unicorn was left without kindness and care and love it would not flourish – it would become ill.

He gazed at the pictures and let his mind wander among them. It all seemed to make sense.

Danni left the library with his head sparkling with ideas and images.

He wanted to show the book to Tim O'Brien and Gary and Kate at the City Farm. He wanted to point to it and make them understand that Moonshine wasn't a sick old horse – Moonshine was a unicorn. She needed to escape to a place of beauty and love and kindness. She needed soft words and... music maybe? Or some of those library books? Or more stroking and singing? Then she would flourish and become her real self: a unicorn.

He could hardly wait for Saturday when he would see Moonshine again. He planned what he would do to cure the horse. He imagined her becoming better and better, stronger and stronger. He imagined her shining.

But first he had to get through Wednesday... and Thursday... and Friday... Each dreary day seemed longer than the last.

The school week passed in the usual blur of unhappiness. Danni kept his head down. He hid. He hoped. On a good day, the KKKs forgot about him and left him alone. On a bad day they noticed him. Then all day he would dread that mad scurry home.

Chapter 10

Saturday came at last. No school. And a chance to go to the Farm Park – a chance to visit Moonlight.

As Danni came into the Farm, Gary and Kate – the helpers – saw him coming in. They didn't smile or wave a greeting as they usually did. They seemed to be avoiding Danni's eyes. Gary gave an uneasy cough, went into the office and came out with Tim.

What was going on?

"Ah Dan," said Tim. He looked uncomfortable.

"I want to talk to you. Come into the office. Sit down."

✰✰✰

Another helper was busy in the corner of the office. Tim nodded a sign to her and she gasped "oh", nodded and slipped out the door. Something was going on.

What?

Danni sat down. Quiet, obedient. Perhaps if he did exactly what he was told, the trouble wouldn't happen. But he could feel trouble gathering in the air. He shivered.

Tim cleared his throat and spoke. "You did a great job with Old Stump.... with Midnight... Moonlight. You really made a difference. Everybody says so. No one could have done more... We all agree you were wonderful with her..."

What? What? WHAT? Danni thought.

"But..."

But *what?*

"...but I'm sorry to tell you that she passed away last night."

What?

Danni stared blankly.

"She's gone."

Gone where?

Tim looked down at his feet. "She's dead. I'm sorry, Dan. It was bound to happen. We couldn't do any more for her... You're still welcome to come here. We have many other animals you can work with. There are the goats... ducks..."

✶⚝✶

Danni stood up so suddenly, the chair fell over behind him. He was out of the office and out of the farm before anyone could say another word to him and he was running, running, running back towards his block of flats.

In the flat he went straight for the exercise bike, and pedalled and pedalled until sweat broke out on his head. Then he pedalled some more. He wanted to pedal until his heart stopped hurting, until his head grew clear.

Chapter 11

On Monday, back at school, it was more of the usual. By home time, Danni had had more than enough. But he was never the first to run out of the gates. He hung around waiting for the coast to clear, checking it was safe.

The slamming of doors, the sound of running feet, the laughs and the voices gradually died away and Danni emerged cautiously, peering around him like an animal edging out of its shelter.

He walked across the now-empty playground and slipped out of the gates. Head down, he scuttled for the safety of the library. His refuge.

Outside, they were there, the KKKs. Waiting, hanging around by the bus stop, bored.

They got the scent of Danni.

Now for some fun.

"Let's get him!" Danni heard, and the chase was on.

Danni ran. He scuttled like an insect trying to find a place to hide, plunging down narrower and narrower streets, alleys, dead ends, past dustbins, backs of buildings, fences, walls, railings. The more he ran, the more they pursued, as if they were all playing parts in some game.

He thrust himself through smaller and smaller gaps, into darker and darker spaces, down concrete rat-runs, but they were always just behind him. He gained the walkways of his block and panted up the stairs. His heart was pounding, his lungs were burning, legs shaking, and in his head he was shrieking. His nightmares of being pursued were being made real again by this chase.

Then, *bang,* he was in, safe behind his own front door. He locked it. Bolted it. Shut them out. And shut himself in.

⁂

That night he could not sleep. He was afraid of closing his eyes. Each time his heavy eyelids closed he jerked awake, afraid of the dark and aware of each sound coming from the street, afraid he might sink back into his nightmare.

In the end he had to give in to sleep, and his eyes closed.

Harsh words, cat-calls, tyres screeching, a sudden series of crashes, glass breaking.

These were the sounds that seeped into his dreams, that surrounded him as he drifted into an uneasy sleep.

Chapter 12

When he woke, the yellow street light was gone. The night sky was velvet black, scattered with tiny diamond splinters. The moon was a sliver of silver.

Danni knelt at the window to look.

Moonbeams transformed everything they touched.

Railings glinted like angel spears.

The walkways gleamed like rivers of silver. Danni breathed in the peace and stillness.

"Wherever my mother is, she will see the same sky," Danni thought. "Wherever my family is, they will be under the same moon." And he gazed and gazed, soaking up the peace, listening to the silence.

He could hear the sound of his own heart, his breathing – and a thrubbing like a drumbeat running through everything.

Something was running along the walkways. Steadily, steadily it came, the faint sounds growing louder and louder, nearer and nearer – a *clip-clopping* noise. A horse? Here?

It came into sight. Eerie, unexpected, elegant, it shone. Its hooves caught the moonlight, its mane shone silver. It stood still, breathtaking in its beauty. Danni stared, dazzled by its brilliance.

What was that on its head? A rope? A shell? A spear?

It was then Danni recognised the creature as the one he had seen in the pages of the library book.

It was a unicorn.

It was Moonlight!

But it was a Moonlight transformed, touched by magic. She held her head high and proud, she stepped lightly, almost gliding, and with every movement her mane shimmered, the unicorn horn gleamed.

She came towards him.

She was so close now, Danni could see her cloud-forming breath. He could smell her sweet breath - wafts of warm hay and grass-green fields and blue sky drifted towards him. He could feel the soft breath warming him.

Danni could reach out now and touch her head. Gentle brown eyes looked back at him – eyes soft with kindness and wisdom – and understanding.

Danni touched the unicorn's lamb-soft ears.

He patted her head, warm and soothing to the touch.

He touched her back, strong, soft, warm and inviting.

Then he was on her back – a bareback rider, with no sense of danger or fear.

He felt the strength beneath him. Felt the muscles ripple as the unicorn started to move — a walk, a trot, a canter, a gallop gallop gallop.

Each step grew lighter, her hooves hovering over the ground in a step, a touch, so light — they were almost floating.

The wind rushed past him — and he was off, racing over roofs, sparks of silver all around him. His imagination took wing and he flew...

He flew.

High over the houses.

Far above the grey streets.

The people below shrank to toys, then ants, then specks, then nothing.

He touched the stars, leapt over moonbeams, raced the wind...

Chapter 13

Next morning, Danni awoke, he was sparkling. He felt so fresh, so alive, so full of hope. He looked out of his window – but there was no unicorn. It had melted away – like the snowman. Everything was back to normal.

Yet everything felt different.

★ ★ ★

He walked to school with a spring in his step.

All day he felt filled with energy, uplifted by hope. He seemed to understand more. The lessons seemed easier. The language seemed clear. His face, usually furrowed with effort, relaxed into a smile. There was a light in his eyes.

But some things stayed the same.

On the way home they followed him again.

The words began to pound against him

rock-hard, stone-sharp. He began to flinch from them, started to look for an alley he could duck into. He clenched his hands, got ready to run.

It was then that he heard the thrumming sound once more.

Was it the sound of unicorn hooves? Or was it his own heart? He felt a silveriness surrounding him. He felt protected. The sharp words bounced off him. They could not touch him. He had a shield.

Danni walked on steadily, steadily. Behind him, his tormentors maintained the same distance, waiting for their cue to break into a run. But Danni stayed on the main street and walked on quietly. He held his head high and passers-by caught his eye. One old lady glared at the gang following Danni. A buggy-pushing mum tutted at them. The keeper of the kebab shop popped his head out. He nodded to Danni.

Danni felt less alone, he felt powerful.

He was the one who could fly. He was the one who had touched stars and leapt moonbeams. He had heard the stars singing. His three tormentors seemed smaller, younger.

Behind him, with shrugs and boredom, the calls faded away.

Home he went, still smiling, starry-eyed.

On the street, broken glass glittered like diamonds.

Michaela Morgan is a writer and poet for young people.
A collection of her poems was shortlisted for the
BBC Blue Peter Award. She has also been shortlisted
for the Children's Book Award, selected as an
International Reading Association Children's Choice
and has won a United Kingdom Reading Association
award. Her first book for Frances Lincoln was the
picture book *Brave Mouse*. Other recent picture books
are the bestselling *Dear Bunny* for Chicken House
and its sequel *Bunny Wishes*. Michaela also writes
for much older children. She divides her time
between Brighton and the South of France
where she works hard at writing and her
hobbies of dozing and daydreaming.

MORE FICTION FROM
FRANCES LINCOLN CHILDREN'S BOOKS

CHRISTOPHE'S STORY
Nicki Cornwell
Illustrated by Karin Littlewood

Christophe has a story inside him – and this story
wants to be told. But with a new country, a new school
and new language to cope with, Christophe can't find
the right words. He wants to tell the whole school about
why he had to leave Rwanda, why he has a bullet wound
on his waist and what happened to his baby brother,
but has he got the courage to be a storyteller?
Christophe must find a way to break through all these
barriers, so he can share his story with everyone.

ISBN 978-1-84507-521-7

GIVE ME SHELTER
Edited by Tony Bradman

Sabine is escaping a civil war…
Danny doesn't want to be soldier…
What has happened to Samir's family?

Here is a collection of stories about children from
all over the world who must leave their homes and
families behind to seek a new life in a strange land.
Many are escaping war or persecution. All must
become asylum seekers in the free lands of the West.
If they do not escape, they will not survive.

These stories, some written by asylum seekers and
people who work closely with them, tell the story
of our humanity and the fight for the most basic of
our rights – to live. It is a testimony to all the people
in need of shelter and those from safer countries
who act with sympathy and understanding.

ISBN 978-1-84507-522-4

PURPLE CLASS AND THE FLYING SPIDER
Sean Taylor
Illustrated by Helen Bate
Cover illustration by Polly Dunbar

Purple Class are back in four new school stories!
Leon has managed to lose 30 violins, much to the
horror of the violin teacher; Jodie thinks she has
uncovered an unexploded bomb in the vegetable patch;
Shea has allowed Bad Boy, Purple Class's guinea pig
to escape; and Ivette has discovered a scary flying spider,
just in time for Parent's Evening!

ISBN 978-1-84507-627-6

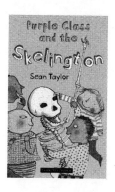

PURPLE CLASS AND THE SKELINGTON
Sean Taylor
Illustrated by Helen Bate
Cover illustrated by Polly Dunbar

Meet Purple Class – there is Jamal who often forgets
his reading book, Ivette who is the best in the class
at everything, Yasmin who is sick on every school trip,
Jodie who owns a crazy snake called Slinkypants,
Leon who is great at rope-swinging, Shea who knows
all about blood-sucking slugs and Zina who makes
a rather disturbing discovery in the teacher's chair…

Has Mr Wellington died? Purple Class is sure he must
have done when they find a skeleton sitting in his chair.
Is this Mr Wellington's skelington? What will they say
to the school inspector? Featuring a calamitous cast
of classmates, the adventures of Purple Class will
make you laugh out loud in delight.

ISBN: 978-1-84507-377-0

WASIM ONE-STAR
Chris Ashley
Illustrated by Kate Pankhurst

Wasim wants to be a One-Star swimmer. But when the
day comes to take the plunge, Wasim's up to his neck
in trouble. When Wasim gets ordered out of the pool
for talking to the new boy, Wayne, his chances of getting
his One Star vanish. Will Wasim be a star or must
he wait until next year for his chance to shine?

ISBN 978-1-84507-744-0

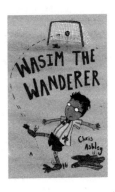

WASIM THE WANDERER
Chris Ashley
Illustrated by Kate Pankhurst

No one at school can score a goal like Wasim!
So he is trying out his football skills for Teamwork 10,000
and that might just lead to a trial with the Woodley
Wanderers! But how can he play his best football
with Robert Bailey lurking around every corner –
and then on the football pitch too?

ISBN 978-1-84507-776-1